THE Baby Tree

SOPHIE BLACKALL

NANCY PAULSEN BOOKS ◉ AN IMPRINT OF PENGUIN GROUP (USA)

NANCY PAULSEN BOOKS
Published by the Penguin Group
Penguin Group (USA) LLC
375 Hudson Street, New York, NY 10014

USA | Canada | UK | Ireland | Australia
New Zealand | India | South Africa | China
penguin.com
A Penguin Random House Company

Library of Congress Cataloging-in-Publication Data
Blackall, Sophie.
The baby tree / Sophie Blackall.
pages cm
Summary: After learning that his parents are expecting a baby, a young boy asks several people
where babies come from and gets a different answer from each before his parents have a chance
to give the right answer. Includes advice on answering questions about reproduction.
[1. Sex instruction for children—Fiction. 2. Questions and answers—Fiction.
3. Babies—Fiction. 4. Pregnancy—Fiction. 5. Humorous stories.] I. Title.
PZ7.B5319Bab 2014   [E]—dc23   2013036309

Manufactured in China by South China Printing Co. Ltd.
ISBN 978-0-399-25718-6
1 3 5 7 9 10 8 6 4 2

Design by Ryan Thomann. Text set in Kamp Friendship.
The illustrations in this book were painted with Chinese ink
and watercolor on Arches hot-press paper.

For Olive and Eggy,
who gave me the idea
in the first place.

After I wake up

and after I get out of bed,

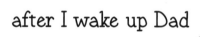

after I wake up Dad

and wake up Mom

and wake up Dad again,

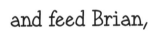 and after I get dressed

and feed Brian,

 we have breakfast.

After breakfast, Mom and Dad
tell me they're going to tell me some news.
And then they tell me the news.
A new baby is coming.

I have a hundred questions in my head,
but the only one that comes out is
Are there any more cocopops?
And because Mom and Dad are all happy
about the baby coming,
they let me have a second helping of cocopops
and I make sure it's a big one.

Then I think of what I really want to know,
which is *Where are we going to get the baby?*
But now Dad's running late,
and Mom's running really late,
and Olive is at the door to walk me to school.

I like Olive because she's a teenager and she knows lots of stuff
and she doesn't make me hold her hand unless I want to
but I usually want to.
So I tell her about the baby.
And I ask her if she knows where babies come from.
And she says, *Sure. You plant a seed and it grows
into a Baby Tree. And then we're at my classroom.*

It's a busy morning,
so I don't think much about the Baby Tree

until after play and snack and rest and reading time,
when we have art.

I try to paint the Baby Tree,
but it doesn't look right.

So I ask Mrs. McClure if she knows where babies come from.

From the hospital, she says,

and then she says,

Boys and girls, it's time to wash our brushes.

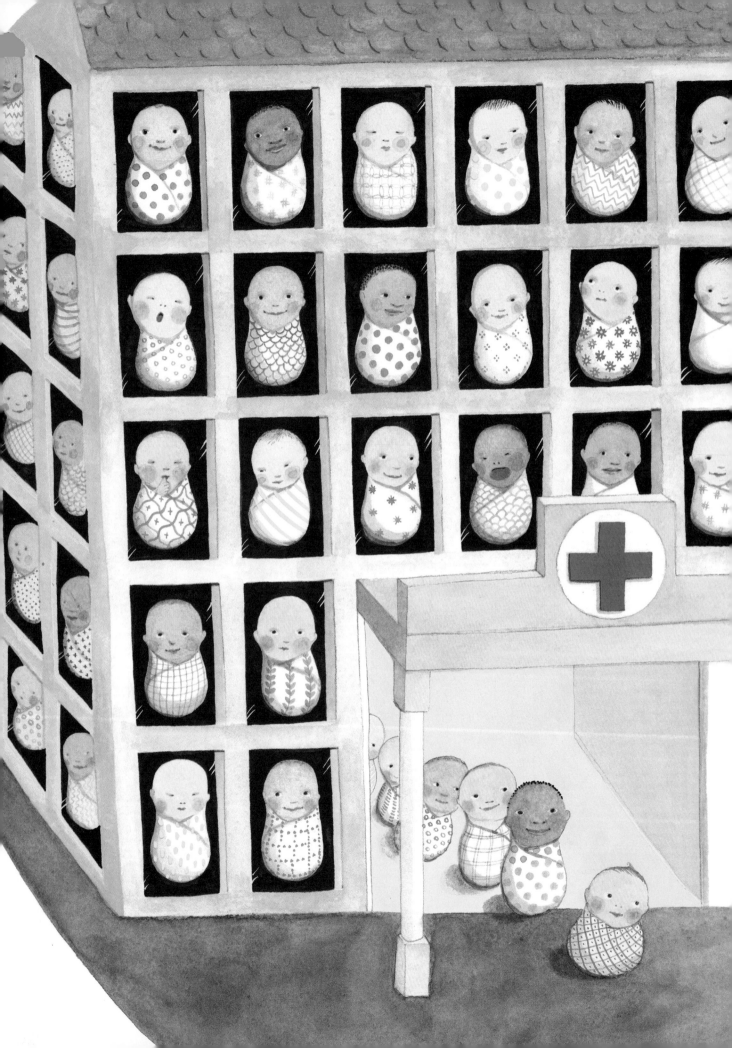

I know for a fact that you only go to the hospital
when you break your leg or when you have
to have something taken out.
Grandpa had stones inside him and he had them taken out
and he keeps them in a jar to show me.
I'll ask Grandpa where babies come from, he'll know.

It's a while before we go to see Grandpa,
and before I can ask him anything,
we have to go up on the roof to visit the pigeons.
When we've let out the polite ones
and are watching them fly around and around in the sky,
I ask Grandpa, *Grandpa, where do babies come from?*

And Grandpa tells me, *A stork brings your baby in the night and leaves it in a bundle on your doorstep.*

I check the doorstep every morning before breakfast but there are no babies, only the mail.

Roberto, the mailman,
thinks babies come from eggs.
But he doesn't know where to get the eggs.

After dinner

 and after my bath

and after my bedtime story

and after my second bedtime story,
I tell Mom and Dad
I have a question to ask them.

And I ask them.
Where do babies come from?

From inside their mom, says Mom.
They start off really tiny, says Dad.

Almost too small to see, says Mom.
They begin with a seed from their dad . . .
Which gets planted in
an egg inside their mom . . .

The baby grows in there
for nine months . . .

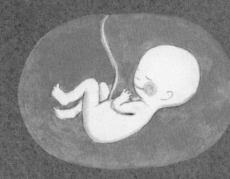

Until it runs out of room . . .
And it's ready to be born.
Sometimes at home . . .
But usually in the hospital.

So, Olive was right about the seed.

And Roberto was right about the egg.

Mrs. McClure was right about the hospital.

But Grandpa . . .
I'm going to have to tell Grandpa where babies really come from.

ANSWERING THE QUESTION *WHERE DO BABIES COME FROM?*

Experts recommend answering your child's questions about reproduction in an honest, age-appropriate way. At around ages 4 to 6 most children want simple answers, and when they are 6 to 8 they may want more details. Here are some suggestions for answering the most common questions about where babies come from in more detail.

How does the seed get from the dad into the mom?

Inside men, there are millions of tiny seeds called sperm. They are too small to see, but under a microscope they look like tadpoles. All babies begin with one sperm and one egg. Usually a man and a woman lie close together and the sperm swims through the dad's penis into the mom's vagina to meet the egg. Of all the sperm, only one can get inside to fertilize the egg, and that's when the baby begins to grow.

How long does it take for the baby to grow?

It takes about nine months for a human baby to grow. In the beginning it looks like a speck and then like a peanut. Around five months it starts to look like a person with fingers and toes and ears and eyes. As the baby grows, the mother's belly gets bigger and bigger each month until the baby is ready to come out.

How does the baby get out?

The mother pushes the baby out through her vagina. Sometimes the baby is not in the right position and a doctor can perform an operation to deliver the baby straight from her belly.

What about twins?

When a mother has two eggs which match up with two sperm, they become fraternal twins. Or, occasionally, a fertilized egg splits in half very early on and identical twins grow side by side.

What about my friend who was adopted?

Even adopted babies begin with a sperm and an egg from what we call their biological father and mother. Sometimes, for all sorts of different reasons, the biological parents can't keep their baby, so another mom and dad choose that baby to love as their own.

What about babies who have two moms or two dads?

A family with two dads or two moms can adopt a baby already born, or one of the moms or one of the dads might be a biological parent. The biological mom will have a sperm donor (a man who gives his sperm) and the biological dad will have an egg donor (a woman who gives her egg). Every family is slightly different, but every single baby begins with a sperm and an egg.